Bella's Rules

by Elissa Haden Guest

pictures by Abigail Halpin

To the splendid Kate Harrison
with special thanks to Gena and Claudia for giving me the idea
E.H.G.

For Caecilia, Eloise, Miriam, and Jude
A.H.

DIAL BOOKS FOR YOUNG READERS
A division of Penguin Young Readers Group
Published by The Penguin Group
Penguin Group (USA) Inc., 375 Hudson Street, New York, NY 10014, U.S.A.
Penguin Group (Canada), 90 Eglinton Avenue East, Suite 700, Toronto, Ontario,
Canada M4P 2Y3 (a division of Pearson Penguin Canada Inc.)
Penguin Books Ltd, 80 Strand, London WC2R 0RL, England
Penguin Ireland, 25 St. Stephen's Green, Dublin 2, Ireland (a division of Penguin Books Ltd)
Penguin Group (Australia), 250 Camberwell Road, Camberwell, Victoria 3124, Australia (a division of Pearson Australia Group Pty Ltd)
Penguin Books India Pvt Ltd, 11 Community Centre, Panchsheel Park, New Delhi - 110 017, India
Penguin Group (NZ), 67 Apollo Drive, Rosedale, Auckland 0632, New Zealand (a division of Pearson New Zealand Ltd)
Penguin Books (South Africa), Rosebank Office Park, 181 Jan Smuts Ave, Parktown North, South Africa, 2193
Penguin China, B7 Jiaming Center, 27 East Third Ring Road North, Chaoyang District, Beijing 100020, China
Penguin Books Ltd, Registered Offices: 80 Strand, London WC2R 0RL, England

Text copyright © 2013 by Elissa Haden Guest
Pictures copyright © 2013 by Abigail Halpin

Designed by Jasmin Rubero
Text set in Jeunnesse Std
Manufactured in China on acid-free paper

1 3 5 7 9 10 8 6 4 2

Library of Congress Cataloging-in-Publication Data

Guest, Elissa Haden.
Bella's rules / by Elissa Haden Guest ; pictures by Abigail Halpin.
p.   cm.
Summary: Bella knows the family rules but lives by her own, as well,
causing her behavior to be "too wild, too rude, and too risky" until Granny brings her a puppy with similar problems.
ISBN 978-0-8037-3393-0 (hardcover)
Special Markets ISBN 978-0-525-42701-8 Not for resale
[1. Behavior—Fiction. 2. Dogs—Training—Fiction. 3. Animals—Infancy—Fiction.
4. Family life—Fiction.] I. Halpin, Abigail, ill. II. Title.
PZ7.G9375Bel 2013   [E]—dc23   2012021516

The illustrations were rendered in watercolor,
graphite, and colored pencil and finished digitally.

ALWAYS LEARNING   PEARSON

This Imagination Library edition is published by Penguin Group (USA), a Pearson
company, exclusively for Dolly Parton's Imagination Library, a not-for-profit
program designed to inspire a love of reading and learning, sponsored in part by The
Dollywood Foundation. Penguin's trade editions of this work are available wherever
books are sold.

Bella knew the family rules by heart.

FAMILY RULES:

No painting on paintings.

No yelling indoors.

And no scaling
the bookcase.

Bella knew the family rules,
but she liked her own rules
much, *much* better.

Bella's Rules:

No washing your hair. Ever.

Except with Mud Shampoo.

Candy for breakfast.

These jellybeans are delish!

Go to Sleep, Bella!

It's too early.
It's too light
out to go to
Sleep.

That's
moonlight!

BELLA

And there is no such
thing as bedtime.

When Sammy the neighbor came to babysit, Bella was sure to point out her rules.

Don't worry, Sammy.

I'm in charge of everything.

Bella built a sculpture out of plates.

She sledded down the stairs.

Your turn, Sammy!

She decorated her parents' bedspread.
And when it was time for bed, Bella explained:

I never sleep, Sammy. Ever.

I'm begging you!

When Bella's parents came home, they had
a serious talk with Bella about her behavior.

It's too wild

said Bella's
father.

Too rude

said Bella's
mother.

Too risky

they said together.

The next day,
Bella wrote a letter.

Dear Sammy,
I'm zorry I
scared you
when I swung
from the

That night Bella's parents placed
a long-distance phone call.

A few days later Granny came to visit.
And she brought a present with her . . .

PUPPY

It was love at first sight.

Bella loved Puppy.

Puppy loved Bella.

When Bella threw a ball, Puppy batted it.

When Bella dropped
a Brussels sprout,
Puppy ate it.

Good
PUPPY!

You're my best friend, Puppy.

And when Bella got in trouble,
Puppy licked her face and made her laugh.

But sometimes Puppy's behavior was **too wild, too rude, and too risky!**

He jumped on Bella
and knocked her down.

That's MY cupcake!

*BAD PUPPY!
TIME OUT
FOR YOU.*

He rolled in the mud
and left footprints
on her bedspread.

And when Puppy wanted to play tug-of-war with Teddy,
Bella had had enough.

anymore,
PUPPY.

Bella's family was right there to help. And little by little, treat by treat, Puppy learned some new rules.

PUPPY'S RULES:

No peeing indoors.

No jumping up
    on the counter.

And no chewing on Teddy.

or Bunny
or blankie

One rainy day Bella taught Puppy a few tricks.

One sunny day Puppy taught Bella a few tricks of his own.

Bella helped Puppy
learn the rules, until
he knew them
by heart.

THAT'S iT, PUPPy!

Of course, every once in a while a rule
is meant to be broken.
And when that happens, it's delicious.